THE STAIN

A SHORT STORY

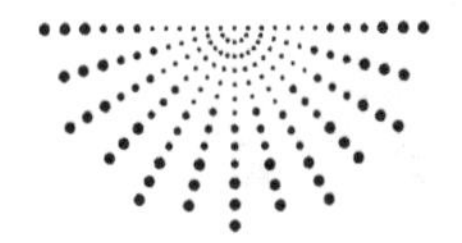

DOUGLAS CLEGG

ALKEMARA
PRESS

PRAISE FOR DOUGLAS CLEGG'S FICTION

"Clegg's stories can chill the spine so effectively that the reader should keep paramedics on standby."
—Dean Koontz, *New York Times* bestselling author.

"Douglas Clegg has become the new star in horror fiction."
—Peter Straub, *New York Times* bestselling author of *Ghost Story* and, with Stephen King, *The Talisman*

"Douglas Clegg is the best horror novelist of the post-Stephen King generation."
— Bentley Little, *USA Today* bestselling author of *The Haunted*.

"Clegg gets high marks on the terror scale…"
—*The Daily News (New York)*

Cover art provided by Damonza.com

ISBN: 978-1-944668-36-5

ALSO BY DOUGLAS CLEGG

STAND-ALONE NOVELS

Afterlife

Breeder

The Children's Hour

Dark of the Eye

Goat Dance

The Halloween Man

The Hour Before Dark

Mr. Darkness

Naomi

Neverland

You Come When I Call You

NOVELLAS & SHORT NOVELS

The Attraction

The Dark Game (Two Novelettes)

Dinner with the Cannibal Sisters

Isis

The Necromancer

Purity

The Words

SERIES

THE HARROW SERIES

Nightmare House, Book 1

Mischief, Book 2

The Infinite, Book 3

The Abandoned, Book 4

The Necromancer (Prequel Novella)

Isis (Prequel Novella)

THE CRIMINALLY INSANE SERIES

Bad Karma, Book 1

Red Angel, Book 2

Night Cage, Book 3

THE VAMPYRICON TRILOGY

The Priest of Blood, Book 1

The Lady of Serpents, Book 2

The Queen of Wolves, Book 3

THE CHRONICLES OF MORDRED

Mordred, Bastard Son (Book 1)

COLLECTIONS

Lights Out: Collected Stories

Night Asylum

The Nightmare Chronicles

Wild Things

BOX SET BUNDLES

Bad Places (3 Novels)

Coming of Age (3 Dark Novellas)

Dark Rooms (3 Novels)

Criminally Insane: The Series (3 Novels)

Halloween Chillers

Harrow: Three Novels (Books 1-3)

Harrow: Four Novels (Books 1-4)

Haunts (8 Novel Box Set)

Lights Out (3 Collection Box Set)

Night Towns (3 Novels)

The Vampyricon Trilogy (3 Novels)

With more new novels, novellas and stories to come.

GET THE NEWSLETTER

Get book updates, exclusive offers, news of contests & special treats for readers—become a V.I.P. member of Douglas Clegg's long-running free newsletter at:

DouglasClegg.com/newsletter

THE STAIN

Jason hunted for the T-shirt just outside the walls of the hotel compound.

He haggled over the price of a particular shirt — the kind Kyle would love. It was boiling hot out; the sea breeze did nothing to cool down the market stall. After an extended back-and-forth with the seller, Jason got a sweet deal: the shirt, flip-flops, plus a few knickknacks for his son's collection.

The guy selling souvenirs under the plastic awning lived — no doubt — among the squalor of hut and shack that ran the length of road between hotel and airport. The man's teeth were a mess. Bright-eyed but malnourished, he sweated in the sauna of noon.

Jason felt a twinge of guilt, having bargained so aggressively just to shave off a buck or two. He recalled his wife's phrase, spoken on their honeymoon a decade earlier, at a coastal resort in that kind of country: “The misfortune of being born in the wrong place.”

Still, Jason closed the deal with American dollars.

The seller chattered in the universal language of pissedness to the short woman who wrapped the items and slipped them into a brown paper bag.

Jason gave the shirt to Kyle the minute he got home from the airport that night.

“LOOK WHAT IT SAYS,” Jason told his son.

Kyle, who was nine, read it out loud.

“Wow,” his son said, after. “Wow.”

“Wow is right,” Jason said. “When you’re a little older, I’ll take you there. It’s got cool cliffs and these islands out in the ocean that you can actually swim to. Your dad parasailed. It’s like flying.”

Over dinner at the sushi place in town, his wife Amy said, “Don’t I get a T-shirt?”

“Maybe next time. I brought in three new clients, one trip.”

“And that means…”

“Well, we can probably put an offer on the beach condo.”

She took a sip of her soda, picked up a chopstick and jabbed it at the air. "Do we really want to do that? We may take a hit for it."

"It's for Kyle, too."

"I think we should just save the money. Invest some more," she said, and reached over to harpoon a piece of dragon roll off his plate. He crossed chopsticks with hers and knocked it back in his court.

"Yeah but a condo, just think," Jason said. "Income property, plus vacations. It'll pay forward. Add a little to our investment portfolio."

"But can we make a business of it?"

"It's a start," he said. "You never know where it might lead."

When they got home, Jason drove the nanny back to her little apartment, paying her double for the extra time.

After Amy fell asleep, Jason went to look in on Kyle.

IN BED, Kyle's head was nearly covered by the blanket. Jason drew the cover down a little, kissing his son on the back of the scalp.

Kyle wore the T-shirt. A slight discoloration ran along the collar where the manufacturer tag had turned upward.

Jason turned on the flashlight of his cell phone to look.

A brown-red stain.

He checked the back of Kyle's neck, but there was no cut.

He wondered if the stain had been there when he'd bought the shirt.

A FEW WEEKS LATER, Jason — at home, contacting potential clients — was interrupted by a call from Kyle's school.

Jason met with the headmistress that afternoon. Her office looked out over the vast grounds with its soccer field and swimming pool. She mentioned Kyle's moods, his disruptive behavior among the other boys, his outbursts.

"But that's why he's here. You're handling it," Jason said.

Then, she mentioned the T-shirt.

"I still don't understand," Jason said.

The headmistress, her eyes a bit too kind, said, "He wears it under his school shirt every day."

"That against the rules?"

"Of course not," she said. "Our nurse suspected he was using it to hide something. We've seen this before."

Earlier that day during recess, one of the

teachers noticed some bruises at Kyle's neck. Boys got bruised all the time, but these seemed odd. Sent him to the school nurse. The nurse noticed that the bruise disappeared down behind the collar of his T-shirt. Kyle told her about having problems sleeping. Waking up in the middle of the night. A scratchy feeling on his back. She asked him to take the T-shirt off. He wouldn't. She had to physically draw it off. He became uncontrollable.

"That's when she saw it," the headmistress said.

"Saw what?"

"The blood. The markings."

Before four, Jason wrangled an appointment with Kyle's pediatrician, who examined the bruises and sores on his back.

"It's nothing — look." The doctor wiped the trace of blood away, and smoothed out the faint scars with his fingers. "I don't think this is anything serious. Just a skin thing."

"How could it happen?" Jason looked from the doctor to his son.

His son looked down at his feet.

"Kyle?" Jason asked.

His son looked up at him. "I told you. I don't know. Maybe I fell. I don't remember."

"Yep, that's probably it," the doctor said. "Probably scraped himself a little. It's not as bad as it looks. See? Might have brushed against something, scratching it. That would account for any blood."

"You sure it's not something worse?" Jason asked.

The doctor would run some tests. He took a little blood, gave an overdue booster shot, suggested a specialist of some kind if it kept up.

"I'm okay," Kyle said. He looked at his father.

"Did anyone hurt you?" Jason asked.

Kyle shook his head. "I already told you a million times."

THAT WEEKEND, Jason and Amy set up camcorders all over the house. They hid them among shelving, behind hanging plants.

Every night, they watched video of the nanny and Kyle from the previous day.

The nanny —from Ecuador — proved efficient for the most part but did push Kyle away when he went to grab a second cookie after he got home from school.

Jason didn't quite like Maria that much after this, but it was hardly cause for firing her.

When asked — frequently — Kyle denied any knowledge of the origin of the bruising and sores.

The bruises faded in a few days.

"My brothers were always bruising themselves," Amy said in bed one night. "Boys play rough. You must've been in a few fights as a kid. That alcoholic school nurse just over-reacted."

The next afternoon, while doing laundry, Jason drew the T-shirt from the hamper.

THE STAIN WAS STILL THERE, right near his son's side. Jason saw a new stain at the collar and another down along the lower part of the shirt, and yet another by the sleeve edge.

He scraped at the stains with his fingernail.

Little dried flecks came up.

He remembered how — as a boy — he once or twice scraped up his side falling off his bike. He'd bruised himself all over after accepting a dare to jump from a boulder. Suspended over a bridge, he'd burned and blistered his hands. No one had ever thought — in those days — to mention it.

Jason bleached the shirt three times, but the stains wouldn't quite come out. He kept seeing them, faint as they'd become.

He threw the shirt out in the trash.

When Kyle discovered it was missing, he slammed his door and told his father he didn't love him.

JASON AND AMY both laughed at this over a drink before bed. "I'm pretty sure I said that to my mother half a dozen times before I was fourteen. Maybe after that, too," she told him. "Don't worry, he still loves you. He's being silly. Maybe we spoil him too much. Your mother thinks so."

Jason didn't respond. He did spoil Kyle, but when he thought of his own childhood, he didn't want Kyle to ever feel the way he felt as a boy — going without when it came to things every boy wanted.

IN BED, finishing up the last of several spreadsheets on her laptop, Amy clicked over to a travel site to book their flight to Costa Rica. "There. We're set."

"When?" Jason asked.

"Two weeks from now. Sun, sand, sea — and vacation home hunt."

In the days leading up to the trip, Jason felt coldness from Kyle — still angry at the loss of his favorite shirt.

JUST BEFORE HUGGING his son goodbye, Jason

promised he'd bring back a bunch of "T-shirts, sunglasses, sandals. Cool stuff."

When the airport limo drove off, Jason looked back, waving from the open window.

Kyle stood in the driveway with Maria.

Kyle turned away a little too quickly, grabbing Maria's hand.

IN COSTA RICA, Jason and his wife spent mornings checking out dozens of condos and houses on the coast. Their afternoons and evenings became bouts of windsurfing, sailing — and drinking a bit too much.

"I don't think I ever want sex again," he laughed after their second go-round in one afternoon.

Every night at seven, they had video chats with Kyle on the laptop. Jason spent a half hour asking him about his day, what he'd done and what friends he'd seen. They'd play a brief game of Turtle Races on the computer before shutting it down. He always let Kyle win.

"You miss him already?" Amy asked.

"Yep. Next time, we'll bring him. It'll be fun. I want to teach him how to wind surf."

"I'd worry he'd drown. You know me. He's too young."

"Plenty old enough to go out on the water —

with me there to catch him. Maybe kayaking, too. That'd be fun."

Amy leaned into him. "Remember when it was always like this? Just the two of us?"

He put his arm around her. "Okay, one more time before shut-eye. Just one more and then this old man's got to sleep."

THEY SETTLED on one of the condos in a colorful complex called Cabeza del Mar.

The property management company was first-rate. A handful of laborers worked on the floors as Amy stepped around them, inspecting their work, suggesting the kitchen appliances.

The agent told them that if they signed the contract soon, they could decide all the upgrades, including the en suite bathroom.

"WE'LL TAKE a few weeks down here a year, rent it out the rest of the time," Jason told Amy over margaritas at their new favorite watering hole. "By the time we're fifty and taking early retirements, it'll be paid off and maybe we'll spend winters here,"

"Or sell it when the market revives," Amy said. "I bet it'll be worth a million then. Maybe more."

"Given what we're going to be paying, it better be more."

They had a goal of reaching eight million dollars in savings and investments — minimum — by the time they were fifty. They looked for new business opportunities whenever they could; that's where Amy's market research skills came into play.

Jason was certain they'd make more than their goal if they were careful. They weren't doing too badly, although they had friends who were doing much, much better.

"Still," Amy said, "Not bad for two kids from the suburbs."

On their last day in Costa Rica, Jason remembered the souvenirs for Kyle. One of the cute little shops near the beach had several T-shirts.

"VERY COOL," Jason said as he sifted through the mountain of shirts, all with printed sayings on the front or back, most of them about the beach and islands and surfing.

"You know, the whole T-shirt industry isn't a bad one," Amy said. "At the company, we've seen growth in this kind of stuff."

"T-shirts? But they're so cheap."

"You'd be surprised. High volume, low costs, high sales. Resorts like this. I'll bet millions of people come through here annually. And every one of them buys a tee, or a beach blanket. A memento, gifts for friends."

"But we're not exactly up on this kind of business."

"One of our clients is in textiles — they have a varied industry, but making cheap clothes is big for them."

"In Malaysia?"

"Various countries," she said, rattling off several, some of which he'd never heard of.

"These are made here, there and everywhere," the shop owner said.

Jason looked over at the wizened old American with mottled skin.

"Little factories," the man said. "Nice clean places, each one of 'em."

"You're from the states," Jason said.

"New York," the man said. "I own this shop and three others down the beach. Run them during high season, on my vacation. I'm in Manhattan most of the year. Started in boxer shorts and went to tees. My wife — died five years, November — used to tell me I'd moved up in the world. Underwear always does well. Resort business is on the upswing."

He went on: in America, in summer, T-shirts were huge. Tourist resorts in Central and South America, year-round profits. Big profit margin, low overhead. "Most people can afford to buy a T-shirt

— a great way to pull in cash. Souvenirs are big. We had shops in Cancun, Mazatlán, Cozumel, along this coast, of course. Miami and San Diego, too. Used to have three shops in Tokyo. Closing most of these, year by year."

"Really," Jason said, looking at the shirts in his hand. "Must be a boatload of work."

"Not these days," the man said. "Overseers run the factories. The accounts are pretty basic. You don't need to have an American down here — or anywhere. You get a local who knows the laws, knows how to crack the whip, so to speak. Here, China, Africa even, India, other parts of Asia, too. Big production, cheap, and a ton of sales. Even online. We've had the biggest growth online. Used to be, I had to fly all the hell over the world to check on factories. Now I just hire these overseers who run these places independently. Throw a rock in any port city and you'll hit some guy just waiting to start up a factory. They take a percentage off the top, including production costs — I don't ever have to worry about it. Everything shows up, inventoried, and everything sells to the point where I don't even discount it. Nothing ever doesn't sell."

After buying several of the shirts, they took the old man out for lunch. Jason and Amy shot a barrage of questions at him from across the table.

LATER, in their hotel suite before checking out, she said, "You really think this is worth doing?"

"Well, we can research it a bit. But I always see people buying souvenirs — and those cheap shirts are popular."

"Everybody has at least one," Amy said.

"And you're always making up funny sayings and stuff."

"True," she said. "It's my one dumbass talent outside of corporate bullshit."

"And we're always talking about diversifying our income."

"Yeah, but there'll be start-up costs."

"Maybe instead of buying a condo, we should create a company. Just a little one."

"Aw, but I loved the condo."

"Sure, but maybe in a year, we'll buy ten condos. Think about it that way."

"But there's a hell of a lot of T-shirts out there."

"We'll differentiate," he said. "We'll do T-shirts just for kids. Or something."

"Sure. We can test it."

"Then, we get them out there," he said. "Get the process going and if it breaks even, fine. If it takes off, we sell it for a big payday within three years. Or less. Who knows? Then, we're not around when it crashes."

~

KYLE WAS THRILLED to get the shirts from Costa Rica. He fell in love with one that had a picture of a palm tree and said, "Fun, Meet Sun."

The boy wore it everywhere.

WITHIN FOUR WEEKS, Amy and Jason got their prototypes up and out. They launched some small online stores with various names, took out banner ads and made a few deals with established vendors.

Jason kept up with the old man on business trips to Manhattan, frequently taking him to lunch and sometimes drinks and dinner, asking him questions, getting advice, until finally the old man said, "When is enough enough? Now's the time. The market's down, but T-shirts are up. If not now, when? Get this going. You'll expand into other areas, once it's running smoothly."

"You don't mind competition?"

"Please. I'm getting out of the business. I'm too old. Time for me to go to my little shops in Costa Rica year-round. Just enjoy sun and my grand-children."

He recommended various regions around the world for the factories, but settled on one or two as sure bets. "You'll get your best bang for your buck, and you'll never have to see it if you don't want."

"Are you kidding? I'd love to see the place where they make our shirts."

"I can't advise that," the old man said. "Let them do their thing, you just do yours."

Still, Jason got on a plane within a week, heading to a small, obscure country the old man recommended.

THE FACTORY WAS a large warehouse thirty miles from the coast.

Jason met the overseer — a local with an unpronounceable name, in his late thirties, smart, educated, confident.

The overseer pointed out the factory floor where the workers would go at it, the bathrooms, his own office, and the machines.

"You'll never have to worry about a thing," the overseer said. "I take care of it all. You'll check spreadsheets and run sales and marketing. And think of this: all the people you're giving jobs to. I thought my little factory would go under, but you're saving it."

Jason had a good trip.

"Production's already begun," he told Amy.

A few weeks later, a problem cropped up.

Kyle.

The nanny was upset, because a woman had

come to the door one afternoon demanding things, bothering her, bothering Kyle when he got home from school.

A neighbor, it seemed, had called the local social service agency.

VISITING SOCIAL SERVICES, Jason met up with the caseworker.

"We got a report," she said, after checking her computer. "Someone noticed your son had scarring around his throat."

Jason stared at her. "What?"

"We didn't find anything wrong with him. We spoke to him. He showed us his neck. It was fine. Still, we had to follow up."

There was a procedure, she told him. She passed him some paperwork. He filled it out.

He wondered if he needed to call his lawyer.

He wondered which neighbor had done this.

THAT NIGHT, Jason sat on the edge of Kyle's bed as his son got into his jammies.

Kyle kept the T-shirt on. Jason asked him to take it off and put on his pajama top.

"But I like to sleep in it."

"I need to wash it. Sleep in another one."

"But this is my favorite," Kyle said.

"Come on, Kyle. Just change into another one. That one's filthy. Stinky." He tried to make the word "Stinky" sound funny so that Kyle would loosen up. But the boy didn't. "You're being stubborn."

"I sleep good in it."

Jason got up and pulled out the middle drawer in the pine dresser by the bed. He reached for a T-shirt. "This is a cool one."

"No."

"Kyle," Jason said. "Just change."

Something came over his son's face. The boy looked as if he were frightened of his father, and embarrassed in a much deeper way than he should have been.

"Kyle, what are you hiding?"

"Nothing."

"Kyle."

His son began crying.

"Kyle, you're being a baby about this."

"I don't want to take my shirt off."

"Why not?"

Kyle looked down at his hands. "I just don't. Don't ask me to."

"Look, one way or another, that shirt is coming off your back. My advice is: just forget all this nonsense. Take it off. Now."

"Please, Dad. Don't make me take it off. Please."

Jason caught his breath. He felt a strange power rising up in his throat. He coughed it back. Breathe. Just breathe. Don't get mad.

"Kyle, look," Jason said, calming. "I'm your best friend, right? And I will never hurt you. Never. But this is important. I think you know why."

"Please," his son whimpered.

Reluctantly, Kyle raised the shirt over his head.

He didn't look at his father when he grabbed the other T-shirt.

"Stop. Freeze." Jason said, just as Kyle began drawing the new shirt down over his neck.

His son stood still.

Jason flicked up the bedside lamp to its highest setting, and lifted off its shade.

The room lit up.

Kyle's side and chest looked bruised. Jason grasped his son's shoulders lightly, turning him around.

The boy's back had a series of crisscross scars raised up in a pattern that made him think of a whipping.

"Holy shit," Jason said. He felt kicked in the gut. "Kyle, what happened?"

Kyle closed his eyes as if he'd dreaded this moment. When he opened them, he looked down at his feet.

"Who did this to you? Was it someone at school?"

Kyle glanced up at his father. He whispered something.

Jason couldn't hear him. He crouched low in front of his son, looking at the scars and bruises.

"Just tell me who did this," Jason said. "I'll take care of it. It won't ever happen again."

"I don't know," Kyle whispered. "I don't know. It just happens."

IN BED WITH AMY, he told her.

"Holy shit," she said.

"Exactly what I said."

She wanted to bolt out of bed and check it out for herself.

Jason told her that would only embarrass Kyle more. "I washed his back. Put some lotion on. He said it doesn't hurt."

"You think it's psychosomatic or something?"

"We'll get him to the doc tomorrow. Don't worry."

"Who the hell is doing this?" she asked.

"It's not Maria, obviously."

"Maybe we need to change schools," Amy said. "If they're not doing something about this…well, maybe they're protecting some little sociopathic bully."

In the morning, when Jason helped get Kyle ready for a trip to the doctor's, he noticed that some of the bruises had faded.

BY THE TIME they got to the doctor's office — and waited another forty minutes for Kyle's pediatrician — the bruises were mostly gone.

The crisscross pattern on the boy's back was barely perceptible when the doctor had Kyle undress.

"Sure, I've seen this sometimes," the pediatrician said. "We don't quite know what it is. Sometimes kids are allergic to stuff. We can test him."

"Allergies," Jason said. "To what? Peanuts?"

"Maybe it's the material. What's this made from?"

Jason shrugged, touching the edge of the material at Kyle's shoulder. "Natural fibers, I think."

"Where's it made?"

"Does that matter?" Jason asked.

The doctor nodded. "Sometimes these factories have other things going on in them. You never know. I've certainly seen this before. Cheap goods, lower standards."

Before he left the doctor's office, Jason set up

two more appointments — one with the child psychiatrist, as recommended by the social worker — and one more to double check the bruises the following week.

~

AFTER KYLE'S session with the psychiatrist, Jason was handed a prescription.

"He seems stressed," the psychiatrist said. "We'll get him on a couple of good meds and see how it goes. He may be a little sleepy after the first dose. If you notice erratic behavior, call me."

"Did he talk about anything I should know?" Jason asked.

"Don't worry about this," she said, ignoring the question. "It'll pass. Get those pills. They'll kick in within a week. I'll bet this clears up by the weekend. I'll call social services about the other thing."

"That's it?"

The psychiatrist nodded. "Bottom line, your son is fine. Kids go through phases. He's not in pain. He's not being bullied. My only concern is that he gets some rest."

~

THAT NIGHT, Jason called the overseer of the factory, who swore up and down that the factory was clean. The workers weren't sick. The fibers were not only natural, but had been tested for allergens.

"Don't worry," his overseer said. "I make shirts for a ton of suppliers. Hell, we make sheets now, we make towels, place mats, scarves, purses — you name it. I've got deals with a lot of great places. You'd be surprised all the stuff we make here." He mentioned several brands to Jason, who noticed — as he went through the house later — that in fact, most of the upholstery was from that region, and the high thread count sheets on the bed were exclusively from this particular factory.

Unable to sleep that night, Kyle crawled in bed with his mother and father.

Given the rough week and the new course of pills that Kyle was on, Jason decided to allow this bending of the rules.

In the morning, after Amy left for her commute, Kyle still snoozed, head on his mother's pillow. He wore a T-shirt that Jason had just thrown out the night before.

Looking at his son's back under the shirt, Jason saw a crisscross of faint scars, bloodstains along them.

He reached out to touch one of the scars. It was

slightly raised. His son flinched, waking up.

"Daddy?" Kyle turned around to look at him. "It happened in my dream again."

"Again?" Jason asked. "What do you mean 'again'?"

Kyle nodded. "That's when I see him."

"Who?"

"The little boy. The one who's hurt." Kyle said. "I dream about him. He says he dreams about me. He likes seeing where we live."

"Bad dreams?"

Kyle nodded. "They beat him."

Thoughts raced through Jason's mind: Kyle was going to tell him the truth. He was going to tell him it was a dream, but it was really and truly the truth. His son was going to tell him now who had done this.

It was no allergy. No psychiatric problem.

Some other boy was hurting him. *A boy in the city. A boy in school. A boy in the neighborhood.*

"Who beats him?" Jason asked.

"Others."

"Who are the others?"

His son squinted and tilted his head slightly.

"You can trust me," Jason said, almost frightened of what his son might say. "Have these 'others' threatened you?"

Kyle shook his head, slowly.

"Tell me what happens in the dream."

"The boy gets hurt. The others make him hurt."

"And who are they?"

"People," Kyle said.

"Do they live near us?"

Kyle shook his head.

"Please, son. This is important. Tell me more about the boy."

"He's not fast enough."

Jason remembered all the bullies in gym class from his own childhood, the boys who just liked to pummel other kids.

"Is the boy not a fast runner? Or good at basketball?"

"Not fast enough," Kyle said. "They make him bleed. They make him cry. Sometimes he can't sleep for days. He's afraid they might kill him."

Unable to control himself, Jason nearly leapt for his son, grabbing him in a bear hug.

"Daddy? Are you okay?"

"Nobody's ever going to hurt you. Nobody," Jason whispered. "You just need to tell me. You need to trust me. I'm your father. I love you. I love you no matter what you do, no matter who you are. You could do the most terrible thing in the world, Kyle, and I would love you anyway. I will love you until the world comes to an end, Even after that, I'd still love you."

Kyle struggled against his father's embrace, but then he began crying, too.

"You're scaring me," he said.

Jason let go. He took a few heavy breaths, calming.

After a minute, Kyle told him more about the boy and what he remembered from the dreams — the bruises on the boy, the scars on his back and shoulders, even the name.

"I think it's his name. I'm not sure he told me. But I think this is his name."

AFTER PULLING Kyle into another school — a better, more expensive one — Jason banned all T-shirts from the house.

KYLE HAD some minor side effects from the course of medication he was on, but slept through most nights. He seemed better behaved and more alert during the day.

The bruising and scarring became a distant memory.

The dreams of the boy hurt by others no longer happened, according to Kyle.

~

THE SIDE BUSINESS of T-shirts took off. Within two years, a buyer approached Jason and Amy about buying the whole operation from them.

Amy felt the offered price was too good not to sell.

Before the sale, they'd take one last trip down to the shirt factory, give a big fat bonus to the overseer and the office workers, and then a great "goodbye" bonus to every single worker on the floor.

IT WAS a big day at the factory, which had grown into three large buildings.

Amy commented on the efficiency of the operation. Jason marveled at the ambitious production schedule; the blocks of apartments for the workers; the canteen; the offices. The overseer and his secretary took them to the little area where their shirts were manufactured.

The line workers remained busy, down on the floor, a humming hive moving in and around a variety of machines. There were several older women, some middle-aged, at least one expectant mother among them. The men were younger, some of them in their teens.

Jason was surprised to see children there, too, running errands, sewing, cutting fabric, rolling it out.

He knew this was the standard of the country, and even children needed to bring money home to their poor families. He didn't love seeing it and mentioned it to the overseer.

"Only fifteen and up in my factory," the overseer said with pride. "The laws here allow for much, much younger. Children need work, just like anyone else, but some of these boys come from families with nothing. Absolutely nothing. It's a pleasure to find some kind of work for their children."

"They look too young." When Jason said this, he felt Amy's elbow in his side.

"We're short, young-looking people," the overseer's secretary said. "Not tall and strong like you people."

All of this did little to reassure Jason. He and Amy exchanged glances.

They went around to the happy and grateful employees, many of whom wept when they were handed cash.

The boys — they seemed not much older than Kyle — came up, grinning, thanking, speaking the few words of English they knew. The girls at the machines kept their eyes downcast, but thanked both of them for the money.

One little boy — could he have been fourteen? He was Kyle's height, but much thinner. He ran up and hugged them both, speaking bad English, thanking them but not daring to look up at their faces.

Jason felt an unexpected tug at his heart. He gave the boy double the amount.

The boy wore one of their T-shirts, the one that Kyle had loved back when he was allowed to wear it.

As the boy turned to run back to his station, Jason saw the crisscross bloodstain marks along his back where the shirt had been torn.

He remembered seeing a long strip of thick cowhide hanging above the door of the overseer's office. When Amy had mentioned it, the secretary remarked that it was hers "so I can whip the boss into shape when he gets lazy."

They all had a good, polite laugh at this.

"You gave him too much," the overseer said, mentioning the boy by name as he ran off among the aisles of machinery. "He's a daydreamer. Never fast enough, never on top of his work. I don't know why I keep some of them on."

"You have a big heart," his secretary said.

Jason recognized the name of the boy.

JASON FELT LOST for the rest of the tour through the factory. He could not look Amy in the eye, nor did he manage much in the way of conversation with the others.

He canceled dinner but nodded when Amy said she wanted to go as a final thank you to the overseer and his secretary. She was sorry he felt ill.

Jason went to lie down in their hotel room.

Amy returned from dinner, very excited, and woke him at midnight.

"Oh my god, Jason, you wouldn't believe it. I think we can make a killing with high-end sheets and pillowcases. We all crunched numbers tonight. They showed me some printouts regarding the competition. He can bring it in under budget. He told me that our business made him rich enough to keep expanding product lines and now…"

She kept talking about the millions they could make and maybe even attach it to a celebrity and market it through some big box stores to appeal to middle-class people who wanted great bedding.

He felt as if he were gasping for air with every word she spoke.

He ran his fingers along bruises at his throat, and felt the skin of his back rise slightly to meet the edge of the whip.

~

ABOUT THE AUTHOR

Douglas Clegg is the *New York Times* bestselling and award-winning author of *Neverland, The Priest of Blood, Afterlife*, and *The Hour Before Dark*, among many other novels, novellas and stories. His first collection, *The Nightmare Chronicles*, won both the Bram Stoker Award and the International Horror Guild Award. His work has been published by Simon & Schuster, Penguin/Berkley, Signet, Dorchester, Bantam Dell Doubleday, Cemetery Dance Publications, Subterranean Press, Alkemara Press and others.

A pioneer in the ebook world, his novel *Naomi* made international news when it was launched as the world's first ebook serial in early 1999 and was called "the first major work of fiction to originate in cyberspace" by *Publisher's Weekly*, covered in *Time* magazine, *Business Week, Business 2.0, BBC Radio, NPR, USA Today* and more. His book *Purity* was the first to be published via mobile phone in the U.S. in early 2001.

He is married, and lives and writes along the coast of New England.

Find the Author Online:

www.DouglasClegg.com

Printed in the USA
CPSIA information can be obtained
at www.ICGtesting.com
CBHW030850240924
14835CB00067B/206